D1418542

Phonics Friends

# Jamal's Job
## The Sound of J

The Child's World

*By Cecilia Minden and Joanne Meier*

Published in the United States of America
by The Child's World®
PO Box 326
Chanhassen, MN 55317-0326
800-599-READ
www.childsworld.com

A special thank you to Darion Nicholson for his performance of "Jamal."

The Child's World®: Mary Berendes, Publishing Director

Editorial Directions, Inc.: E. Russell Primm, Editorial Director and Project Editor; Katie Marsico, Associate Editor; Judith Shiffer, Associate Editor and School Media Specialist; Linda S. Koutris, Photo Researcher and Selector

The Design Lab: Kathleen Petelinsek, Design and Page Production

Photographs ©: Photo setting and photography by Romie and Alice Flanagan/Flanagan Publishing Services: cover, 4, 14, 16, 18, 20; Corbis: 10; Getty Images/digitalvision: 12; Getty Images/The Image Bank/Felix Clouzot: 6; Getty Images/Photodisc Blue: 8.

**Library of Congress Cataloging-in-Publication Data**
Minden, Cecilia.
  Jamal's job : the sound of J / by Cecilia Minden and Joanne Meier.
    p. cm. — (Phonics friends)
  Summary: Jamal's father, mother, brother, sister, and even Jamal  have different jobs, in simple text featuring the "j" sound.
  ISBN 1-59296-297-1 (library bound : alk. paper)
  [1. English language—Phonetics. 2. Reading.] I. Meier, Joanne D. II. Title. III. Series.
PZ7.M6539Jam 2004
  [E] —dc22                                    2004002198

**Note to parents and educators:**
The Child's World® has created Phonics Friends with the goal of exposing children to engaging stories and pictures that assist in phonics development. The books in the series will help children learn the relationships between the letters of written language and the individual sounds of spoken language. This contact helps children learn to use these relationships to read and write words.

The books in this series follow a similar format. An introductory page, to be read by an adult, introduces the child to the phonics feature, or sound, that will be highlighted in the book. Read this page to the child, stressing the phonic feature. Help the student learn how to form the sound with her mouth. The Phonics Friends story and engaging photographs follow the introduction. At the end of the story, word lists categorize the feature words into their phonic element. Additional information on using these lists is on The Child's World® Web site listed at the top of this page.

Each book in this series has been carefully written to meet specific readability requirements. Close attention has been paid to elements such as word count, sentence length, and vocabulary. Readability formulas measure the ease with which the text can be read and understood. Each Phonics Friends book has been analyzed using the Spache readability formula. For more information on this formula, as well as the levels for each of the books in this series please visit The Child's World® Web site.

Reading research suggests that systematic phonics instruction can greatly improve students' word recognition, spelling, and comprehension skills. The Phonics Friends series assists in the teaching of phonics by providing students with important opportunities to apply their knowledge of phonics as they read words, sentences, and text.

This is the letter *j*.

In this book, you will read words that have the *j* sound as in:

*job, jets, jacket,* and *jar.*

Jamal wishes he had a job.

Jamal's dad has a job.

He can fly big jets.

His mom is a dance teacher.

She jumps and kicks.

His brother, Jake, is a cook.

He wears a special white jacket.

His sister, Jasmine,

works in a shop.

She sells jars of candy.

"I wish I had a job," says Jamal.

"Maybe I can join the circus.

I would enjoy joking around."

"I'm too young to join the circus.

I would miss my family."

"We have a job for you," says Dad. "Your job is to just be you!"

# Fun Facts

If you want an exciting job when you grow up, consider being a wild animal trainer. This job involves working both with animals and the public, and it requires a lot of courage! Animal trainers who work at zoos and aquariums deal with everything from killer whales to lions and tigers. This job can be dangerous, but it can also be a lot of fun. Trainers sometimes work in Hollywood if a wild animal is performing in a movie.

German scientists flew the first jet plane in 1939. Certain jets can fly at speeds greater than 760 miles (1,223 kilometers) per hour—this is faster than the speed at which sound travels! The term *jumbo jet* describes a jet that was designed to seat about 500 passengers. A pilot flew the first jumbo jet in 1970.

# Activity

### Just Thinking about Jobs

You have a while before you need to decide what your job will be, but you can start investigating different jobs now. If you know someone who has a job you think you might enjoy, ask if you can visit her at work one day. If you can't do that, ask her if the two of you can talk about her job. You can also visit the library and check out books about different jobs that interest you.

# To Learn More

## Books

### About the Sound of J
Klingel, Cynthia, and Robert B. Noyed. *Jump!: The Sound of J.* Chanhassen, Minn.: The Child's World, 2000.

### About Jets
Jefferis, David. *Jets.* Austin, Tex.: Raintree Steck-Vaughn, 2001.
Pallotta, Jerry, and Rob Bolster (illustrator). *The Jet Alphabet Book.* Watertown, Mass.: Charlesbridge Publishing, 1999.

### About Jobs
Glassman, Peter, and Timothy Bush (illustrator). *My Dad's Job.* New York: Simon & Schuster Books for Young Readers, 2003.
Marshall, James. *Fox on the Job.* New York: Dial Books for Young Readers, 1988.

### About Jokes
Rosenberg, Pam, and Patrick Girouard (illustrator). *Dinosaur Jokes.* Chanhassen, Minn.: The Child's World, 2004.
Rosenberg, Pam, and Patrick Girouard (illustrator). *Knock-Knock Jokes.* Chanhassen, Minn.: The Child's World, 2004.

## Web Sites

### Visit our home page for lots of links about the Sound of J:

*http://www.childsworld.com/links.html*

Note to Parents, Teachers, and Librarians: We routinely check our Web links to make sure they're safe, active sites—so encourage your readers to check them out!

# J Feature Words

## Proper Names
Jake

Jamal

Jasmine

## Feature Words in Initial Position
jacket

jar

jet

job

join

joking

jump

just

## Feature Word in Medial Position
enjoy

# About the Authors

*Cecilia Minden, PhD, directs the Language and Literacy Program at the Harvard Graduate School of Education. She is a reading specialist with classroom and administrative experience in grades K–12. She earned her PhD in reading education from the University of Virginia. Cecilia and her husband Dave Cupp enjoy sharing their love of reading with their granddaughter Chelsea.*

*Joanne Meier, PhD, has worked as an elementary school teacher and university professor. She earned her BA in early childhood education from the University of South Carolina, and her MEd and PhD in education from the University of Virginia. She currently works as a literacy consultant for schools and private organizations. Joanne Meier lives with her husband Eric, and spends most of her time chasing her two daughters, Kella and Erin, and her two cats, Sam and Gilly, in Charlottesville, Virginia.*